Heather Dyer grew up in North Wales. Her family moved to Canada when she was eight, where they lived for a time in a log cabin. Heather works as an editor and teaches writing at Aberystwyth University, where she is also studying for a PhD.

Her books for children have received several awards. *The Girl with the Broken Wing* was one of Richard and Judy's 'Best Children's Books Ever', *The Boy in the Biscuit Tin* was nominated for the Galaxy Best British Children's Book A~~~~ *Fish in Room 11* won the ~~~~ ~~~~ward.

Chloe Douglass gr ~~~~ ~~~~u on the Welsh Border, a ~~~~ surrounded by myths and legends. She was forever drawing dragons, unicorns and mountainous landscapes. Chloe graduated from Kingston University with an MA in Illustration in 2012 and has been creating stories and characters since then. She also produces her own greeting cards.

She lives in Wimbledon with her two fluffy cats, and when not illustrating she can be found singing at her local community choir, gardening, drinking an impressive amount of earl grey tea and sewing felt por~~~~

For Elinor,
whose bedroom flew.
Heather

For Mam, Dad and Pedro,
thanks for the unwavering support!
Chloe

The Flying Bedroom

Heather Dyer

Illustrated by
Chloe Douglass

Firefly

First published in 2014
by Firefly Press
25 Gabalfa Road, Llandaff North, Cardiff, CF14 2JJ
www.fireflypress.co.uk

Text © Heather Dyer 2014
Illustrations © Chloe Douglass 2014

A CIP catalogue record of this book is available from the British Library.

The author wishes to acknowledge the award of a New Writer's Bursary from Literature Wales for the purpose of starting this book.

Print ISBN: 978-1-910080-02-3
Epub ISBN: 978-1-910080-03-0

Typeset by: Elaine Sharples

Printed and bound by: Bell and Bain, Glasgow

Contents

The Flying Bedroom and the Snowman – 1

The Flying Bedroom and the Island – 15

The Flying Bedroom at the Theatre – 29

The Flying Bedroom in Outer Space – 43

The Flying Bedroom and the Pirates – 55

The Flying Bedroom and the Train – 68

This is Elinor's bedroom. It looks ordinary.

But it's not.

The Flying Bedroom
and the Snowman

Snow was falling over Aberdovey. Outside, through the dusk, large feathery flakes settled on the empty gardens and the quiet roads.

'It looks like it's sticking,' said Elinor's mother.

When Elinor went to bed it was still snowing.

'If it carries on,' said Elinor, 'will there be enough to build a snowman?'

'Perhaps,' said Elinor's father.

Elinor lay awake for a long time, watching snowflakes flurrying like moths around the street lights. But eventually she closed her eyes and slept.

And while she slept, her bedroom flew.

Round and round and up and down went Elinor's bedroom. Snowflakes swirled overhead. A balled-up sock rolled off the edge of Elinor's bedroom and was lost forever. One of Elinor's drawings blew off the wall and was carried up, up and away…

And then down, down, down went Elinor's bedroom until with a 'bump!' and a long, slow slide, it stopped.

Elinor opened her eyes. Her bedroom ceiling

and her outside wall had disappeared, and the sky was crowded with snowflakes. Elinor put on her rabbit slippers and her dressing gown and went to the edge of her bedroom. The snow was falling thickly. 'Hello?' she called. 'Is anyone there?'

There was no reply.

Elinor made a snowball and threw it into the blizzard.

'Ow!' said someone.

'Oh!' said Elinor. 'Sorry!'

Out of the blizzard came a portly figure. He was wearing a black top hat and a red wool scarf and his arms were sticks with mittens on the end. He had two lumps of coal for his eyes, a carrot for his nose, and a pipe stuck in his mouth.

'Are you all right?' asked Elinor.

'I've been worse,' said the snowman. He was rolling along from side to side, leaving a channel in the snow behind him. He came to the edge of

Elinor's bedroom and with a wag of his twiggy arms he rolled right in across the threshold.

'Whew!' he said. 'What a day!' He took off his hat and his scarf and threw them on the chair. 'Nice place you've got here.'

'Thanks,' said Elinor.

'Mind if I stop a while and thaw out a little?'

'Not at all. Is it cold out there?'

'Cold? It's freezing! But that's not the worst of it.'

'It isn't?'

'No. The boys are the real problem.'

'The boys?'

'Throwing stones,' the snowman said, 'and smashing things. You know what I mean?'

4

Elinor did.

The snowman took his pipe out of his mouth and knocked it on Elinor's chest of drawers. A little lump of snow dropped out onto the carpet and began to melt.

'Warm in here, isn't it?' said the snowman. His carrot nose was no longer sticking straight out but pointing downwards.

'You don't think it's a little *too* warm,' said Elinor cautiously, 'for someone like yourself?' She had noticed that where the snowman stood, a large damp patch was spreading.

'Too warm? Not at all! Good for you, a bit of heat. Sweats out the impurities.'

'It's just,' said Elinor anxiously, 'that I wouldn't like you to – you know – *melt* or anything.'

'Nonsense!' said the snowman. His words were getting slushier. 'I'm like my gwandfather.'

'Your what?'

'My Gwandfather. He loved the heat. Lived in India.'

'In *India*?'

'Met my gwandmother on the twain.'

'On the what?'

'Twain! Twain!' said the snowman. 'Chug-a-lug-lug!'

'Oh! *Train*,' said Elinor.

The snowman creaked and seemed to shift a little. Elinor got a towel and pressed it on the damp patch. While she was doing this, the snowman's pipe fell out. Elinor stuck it in again.

'I sink I'll shtay a little longer,' the snowman said. 'I like it here.'

'I wouldn't stay *too* long,' said Elinor.

'Why not?'

'You might begin to – oh!' One of the snowman's coal eyes fell out and rolled across the carpet. Elinor went after it.

'Whatsa matter?' said the snowman.

'Your eye!'

'Wot?' said the snowman. 'Stand where I can shee you!'

'Hold still!' Elinor pressed the coal back into the snowman's head, where it sat more deeply than it had before.

'Ah! There you are!' said the snowman. 'And look! It's stopped snowing.'

And so it had. The sky had cleared. The sun was shining and the snow lay still and sparkling as far as the eye could see.

'P'rhaps,' said the snowman, 'I should be going.'

But just then there came a knock at the window – and there was the snowman's wife, wearing a paisley headscarf and a pair of sunglasses. 'There you are!' she cried. 'Sitting here melting while I'm out looking for you!'

'Oh dear,' said the snowman.

His wife rolled in across the threshold. 'Look at the state of you!'

'I'm sorry,' said Elinor. 'I tried to tell him but—'

'It's not your fault,' said the snowman's wife. 'He's always doing this. Let's get him up.'

The snowman put out his twiggy arms, and Elinor and the snowman's wife took hold of them and pulled. But the snowman's arms came right off in their hands. They stuck them in again.

'Let's push from behind,' said Elinor. So they went behind and pushed, and the snowman rocked slushily across the carpet and out into the snow again.

But he was only half the snowman that he had been. His head slumped, his eyes were lopsided and he had lost his nose and two of the buttons on his front.

'Oh dear!' said his wife.

'Oomph umph,' said the snowman.

The snowman's wife put a mitten to her mouth and began to cry.

Just then there were voices – and over the brow of the hill came several figures bundled up in scarves and hats and winter boots.

'Oh *no*!' said the snowman's wife. 'It's those boys again.'

The boys were laughing and throwing snowballs at each other.

'HEY!' yelled Elinor. 'Hello! Could you give us a hand?'

The boys came over.

Carefully, Elinor removed the snowman's two coal eyes, his pipe, and his remaining buttons, and handed them to the snowman's wife. Then she pulled off the snowman's twiggy arms and stood them in the snow like little trees. She picked off his remaining buttons one by one. Eventually there was nothing left of the snowman but two snow balls – a small one for his head and a big one for his body.

'First the head,' said Elinor, and she pushed the snowman's head right off so that it fell – *plut* – into the snow. Then she began rolling it away. As she rolled it through the snow it got bigger and rounder and by the time she had rolled it back again, it was twice the size it had been.

'Now the body,' said Elinor.

The boys helped Elinor roll the big ball in a circle. The further they rolled it the bigger it got and by the time they had rolled it back again it was twice the size it had been. Then Elinor and the boys lifted the snowman's head back on his body. Elinor replaced the snowman's eyes, his carrot nose, his pipe, his buttons and his twiggy arms, and before long the snowman was as good as new – better, even.

'I'm a new man!' said the snowman.

The snowman's wife looked doubtful. 'Don't you think his head's a little big?'

'Not at all!' said the snowman. 'It's perfect. Thanks, lads!'

'You're welcome,' said the boys, and they went off, singing, through the snow.

'What nice boys,' said the snowman's wife.

'Very nice,' agreed the snowman.

Elinor looked at the sky. It had clouded over again, and the first few flakes of snow were beginning to fall.

'We'd better be going,' said the snowman's wife.

'Just a minute,' said Elinor. She went and got the snowman's hat and scarf from her wicker chair.

'Much obliged,' said the snowman. 'Goodbye!'

'Goodbye!' said Elinor.

The snowman and his wife linked arms and went rolling away through the snow. Elinor listened to their voices grow fainter and fainter until they had disappeared altogether. Then she took off her slippers and her dressing gown and climbed back into bed. She lay there for a moment, watching the snowflakes swirling overhead. But eventually she closed her eyes and slept.

When Elinor woke up, her ceiling and her outside wall were back again. It was strangely quiet and her room was filled with pale reflected light. Elinor went to the window and looked out. The sun was shining and all of Aberdovey was white – and there was Elinor's father. He was rolling a huge ball of snow down the middle of the road. Elinor banged on the glass, and her father looked up and waved. 'Come on out!' he shouted. 'I'm building a snowman!'

The Flying Bedroom and the Island

Sunday night was bath night. Elinor hated bath night because it meant school on Monday morning. She stood shivering while her mother rubbed her head with a towel.

'Now go and dry your hair,' said Elinor's mother. 'You mustn't go to bed with it wet.'

'Why not?' said Elinor.

'Because you'll wake up with it sticking out all

over the place – and you don't want that, do

you?'

But Elinor didn't dry her hair. She sat in bed

for a long time, playing Angry Rabbit on her

mother's phone.

'Why aren't you asleep?' said her father.

'You've got school in the morning.'

'I don't want to go to school,' said Elinor.

'I know you don't,' her father said. 'But you

have to. Everybody does.' Then he kissed her

goodnight and switched out the light – and

eventually, with her hair still wet, Elinor fell

asleep.

And while she slept, her bedroom flew.

Elinor's bedroom flew far out across the sea. The

curtains billowed out like sails, and the waves

16

splashed up and wetted the underside of Elinor's room. Straight towards the setting sun flew Elinor's room until it caught up with the morning. Then down it went – *splash!* – into the sea.

Elinor opened her eyes. It was very bright, and where her ceiling had been there was a blue, blue sky. Elinor got out of bed and went to the edge of her room. A small wave slopped up onto the edge of the carpet.

Her bedroom was at sea!

Elinor went to the window and leaned out. A breeze was blowing and Elinor's bedroom began to move. A little wave crested in front, and the water churned up behind.

'Full speed ahead!' cried Elinor.

The wind was getting stronger. A pile of Elinor's school books fell off the back of her

bedroom and were soon left far behind. But
Elinor didn't care. She put on her sun hat and
binoculars.

A long way off she could see a small island
covered in trees. 'Land ahoy!' cried Elinor. She
sailed closer and closer to the island until soon
she could see a girl standing on the beach. There
was a little dog too, barking.

Elinor waved.

The girl waved back.

Straight towards the beach sailed Elinor until, with a grating noise, her bedroom ran aground. Elinor jumped out and waded ashore, and she and the island girl pulled her room up on the sand.

'I'm Elinor,' said Elinor.

'I'm Elle,' said the island girl. 'And this is Monty. I like your room. Can I take a look?'

'Of course,' said Elinor.

So Elle climbed aboard and wandered round,

picking things up and putting them down again. She looked very much like Elinor except she was much browner, and her hair was sticking out all over the place. She flicked through Elinor's books and sat on Elinor's bed and switched Elinor's bedside light on and off and on again. Then she said, 'Do you want to see my house now?'

'What about my room?' said Elinor. 'Will it be all right?'

'Of course it will. Come on!'

So the girls ran off along the beach with Monty in the lead.

Elle's house was just above the tide line. It was made from bits of driftwood and planks salvaged from shipwrecks, and there were shells and green glass pebbles on a shelf.

'It's lovely,' said Elinor.

'I made it myself,' said Elle.

Elinor and Elle crouched inside the house eating ship's biscuits and swigging water out of green glass bottles.

'Do you live here on your own?' asked Elinor.

'Just me and Monty,' said Elle.

The little dog wagged his tail.

Elinor wondered what it must be like, going to bed when you liked, getting up when you liked, doing whatever you wanted all day long. 'It must be wonderful,' she said.

'It is. Do you want to see the rest of my island?'

'What about my bedroom? Are you sure it will be all right?'

'Of course it will. Come on!'

So they explored the forest. Elle showed Elinor a waterfall disappearing into mossy rocks, and a hollow tree big enough to hide inside. Then they climbed a mango tree and sat in the branches eating mangoes and throwing the

22

stones to the ground, while Monty sat at the foot of the tree, barking.

When they were full they climbed down again and washed their hands and faces in a stream. Then they chased Monty along the forest paths, and when they were tired they went up to the lookout point and sat looking out to sea. There was nothing but water in all directions, and the sun was setting low down over the horizon. Elinor told Elle all about Aberdovey and her parents and her friends at school – but it all seemed very far away and hardly real.

'I wish I didn't have to go home,' said Elinor.

'Don't, then,' said Elle.

'I've got to. I've got school tomorrow.'

'Don't go.'

'I have to. Everyone does.'

'I don't,' said Elle.

The sun went down. A chill wind blew. 'It's time I was going,' said Elinor.

But she didn't go. Elle collected small twigs and lit a fire and they sat with Monty between them, watching the flames dance and crackle – and except for Elinor's straw hat and binoculars, they looked so much the same that you could hardly tell them apart.

'It's getting late,' said Elinor.

The stars came out. The sea was black and glittered in the moonlight, and out on the water there was a light – a small orange light – bobbing in the blackness.

'What's that?' said Elle, pointing.

'What's what?' said Elinor.

'That light.'

Elinor looked through her binoculars. Then she jumped to her feet. 'It's my BEDROOM!'

24

'Let me see,' said Elle.

But Elinor was already running back down the hillside, through the forest and along the beach to the place where her bedroom had been. She could see it, floating some way out. Her bedside light was on.

'You don't have to go,' said Elle, catching up with her.

'Yes I do,' said Elinor. But she hesitated. 'Come with me, if you want.'

'Would I have to go to school?' said Elle.

'Yes,' said Elinor.

'And wash my hair?'

'I'm afraid so.'

'Thanks,' said Elle, 'but I think we'd rather stay here.'

So Elinor gave Elle her straw hat and binoculars, and hugged her tight. Then she hugged Monty, too, who licked her.

'Goodbye, then!' said Elinor.

'Goodbye!' said Elle.

Elinor waded in and started swimming. The water was choppy and waves kept splashing in her face – but the light from her bedroom showed her the way. Soon Elinor was close enough to grab hold of the edge of her bedroom. Then, with a kick of her legs – *hup!* – she was up and dripping on the carpet.

She could still see the dark hill of the island, and on the wind came the sound of Monty barking. Elinor switched her bedside light off and on again, to signal that she had arrived. Then she changed into some dry pyjamas, climbed into bed and switched out the light. And eventually, with her hair still wet, she fell asleep.

When Elinor woke up it was morning and her mother was drawing the curtains. Elinor sat up.

'Good grief,' said Elinor's mother. 'Look at the state of your hair!'

Elinor got out of bed and went to look in the mirror. Her hair was sticking out all over the place!

She studied it from the left and from the right.
Then she smiled. She rather liked it.
And so did her friends at school.

The Flying Bedroom at the Theatre

On Thursday, Elinor wasn't well.

'I think you've got a temperature,' her mother said. 'You'd better stay in bed.'

It felt strange being in bed in the middle of the day. Elinor could see daylight round the edges of her curtains and could hear people passing by outside – and next door she could hear Mrs Pritchard sweeping her drive: swish, swish, swish.

But eventually, Elinor closed her eyes and slept.

When Elinor woke up, the ceiling and the outside wall had gone. Where the ceiling had been there were joists and pulleys, and where the outside wall had been there was a heavy velvet curtain. From the other side of the curtain there came a muttering and a rustling.

Elinor sat up. A moment later her bedroom door opened and in came a man with a clipboard. His name badge said: DIRECTOR.

'Is everything all right?' he said.

'No,' said Elinor. 'It's not.'

'What's the matter?'

'I can't sleep. What's that noise?'

'What noise?'

'That muttering and rustling.'

'That's the audience, darling!'

'Can't you make them go away?'

'No I can't! They've paid good money to see you.'

'Me?'

'Yes, you. You're the star of the show!'

'No I'm not,' said Elinor. 'I don't even know the lines.'

The director groaned. 'This is all I need.'

Just then a make-up artiste appeared. When she saw Elinor she gasped. 'Are you all right?' she said. 'You're very pale.'

'No!' said Elinor. 'I'm not all right. I'm—'

'Don't worry,' said the make-up artiste. 'This will do the trick.' And she dusted two red spots on Elinor's cheeks. Then she turned to the director. 'Do you think the light is better over there?' she said.

'Perhaps,' said the director.

The next thing Elinor knew they were pushing her bed across the room.

'Hey!' said Elinor. 'Move it back again!'

'She's right,' said the director. 'It was better where it was before.'

So they pushed it back again. Then the door opened and the king appeared, followed by the queen.

'Is everything all right?' said the king.

'No,' said the director. 'It's not. Sleeping Beauty here has forgotten her lines.'

'But this is the crucial scene!' said the queen. 'This is where you get to kiss Prince Charming and live happily ever after.'

'I don't want to kiss Prince Charming.'

'Did I hear my name?' said a voice, and along came a handsome young man in purple tights. He was followed by a pantomime horse and twenty ballerinas, all on points.

'Ah! Prince Charming!' said the director. 'Thank goodness you're here. Talk to Sleeping Beauty, will you?'

'Why? What's the matter?'

'She's forgotten her lines.'

'I haven't *forgotten* them,' said Elinor. 'I never knew them in the first place.'

'Never knew them?' cried the prince. 'How

very unprofessional!' And then everyone started talking at once.

In the middle of it all, Elinor looked up and saw a plump lady being lowered down from the rafters on a rope. She was wearing pink tights and a tutu and had wings made from tights stretched over coat hangers.

'Ah!' said the director, relieved. 'The fairy godmother's here.'

The fairy godmother smiled. 'Is everything all right?'

'No,' said the director.

'She's forgotten her lines,' said the queen.

The fairy godmother laughed. 'Just make it up as you go, my dear! Improvise!' She tapped the top of Elinor's head with her wand, then was reeled up again.

'She'll do no such thing,' said the director.

He shook the script in Elinor's face. 'You'll stick to your lines, do you hear?'

Elinor had had enough. 'Out!' she said. 'All of you!'

Just then the director's pager buzzed. 'Everybody backstage!' he said. 'Curtain in two minutes!' And they all rushed out and slammed the door.

Relieved, Elinor lay back down and closed her eyes.

For a moment, all was quiet. Then the curtains opened and a bright light shone into Elinor's room. Elinor sat up, blinking, and saw rows and rows of tiered seats filled with ladies with towering hairdos and men in dinner jackets. Her bedroom was at the theatre!

Then the door opened and in came Prince Charming. He ran across and knelt beside Elinor's bed.

'Now what?' said Elinor.

The audience burst out laughing. Prince Charming looked disconcerted for a moment, then he said, 'Sleeping Beauty, I came to wake you from your slumber.'

'I told you,' said Elinor. 'I don't want to be woken.'

The audience laughed again.

'But you've been sleeping for a hundred years,' said the prince. 'It's time to—'

'Go away!' said Elinor.

A man at the front guffawed. Prince Charming hesitated.

'I'm waiting…' said Elinor.

'Fine!' said Prince Charming, and he stomped out, slamming the door behind him.

The audience roared with laughter, and there was a round of applause. But presently, the laughter died down and there was an expectant hush. Elinor looked at the audience. 'You can go home now,' she said.

The audience roared with laughter, but nobody moved.

'The show's over!' said Elinor.

There was more laughter. But still nobody moved. So Elinor got out of bed, marched to one side of the stage, and pulled the curtain across. 'Good night,' she said. Then she went to the other side and drew that curtain, too. But just as she was about to get back into bed the door opened and in rushed the king and queen. They linked their arms in hers and lined up for the final bow – then the curtains parted.

'BRAVO!' cried the audience. 'BRAVO!'

The queen blew kisses and the king took off
his crown and gave a bow. Then in came the
troupe of ballerinas and the pantomime horse

and the fairy godmother and all the rest of the cast. And finally, to thunderous applause, the prince arrived.

People stamped and cheered and threw roses at the stage, and Prince Charming gathered up the roses and tossed them to the ladies in the front row.

Three times the curtains opened and closed. Three times the actors bowed and blew kisses. Then the curtains closed for the very last time.

The director turned to Elinor. 'You were fabulous, darling!'

'I was?' said Elinor.

'You're a natural,' said the fairy godmother.

'I am?' said Elinor.

'Yes,' said the queen. 'Now let's go and eat.'

They all trooped out again, talking and laughing. But Elinor hung back. When everyone had gone she shut her bedroom door. Then, just to be sure, she went and put her head out through the curtains. The last few theatre-goers were leaving through the door marked EXIT and the cleaner was sweeping between the seats.

'Goodnight,' said Elinor.

'Goodnight,' said the cleaner.

Elinor climbed back into bed and eventually, soothed by the swish, swish, swish of the cleaner's broom, she closed her eyes and slept.

Some time later Elinor woke up. Her mother had brought up a tray with a bowl of tomato soup, a slice of white bread – buttered – with the crusts cut off, and a red rose in a vase. 'You've got good colour,' said Elinor's mother. 'How are you feeling?'

'Much better, thanks,' said Elinor.

Elinor's mother said, 'That's fabulous, darling.'

When her mother had gone, Elinor got out of bed and went to the window. She opened the curtains wide and looked out across Aberdovey. Then she gave a bow, and blew the world a kiss.

The Flying Bedroom
in Outer Space

On Friday there was a full moon.

'What do you think it's like,' said Elinor, 'on the moon?'

'A bit dry,' said her father, tucking her in.

Elinor was thoughtful.

'And lonely too, I should think,' her father said. Then he kissed Elinor goodnight and went out, shutting the door behind him.

But he had left the curtains open. A path of moonlight shone over the carpet, up the side of Elinor's bed and across her pillow. Elinor lay awake for a long time, looking at the moon. But eventually she closed her eyes and slept. And while she slept, her bedroom flew.

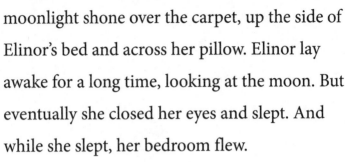

Up and up went Elinor's bedroom until Aberdovey was just a small cluster of lights below. Higher and higher it flew, straight between the moonlit clouds and up, up, out of the Earth's atmosphere altogether.

When Elinor woke up it was very quiet and her bedroom was surrounded by stars. She went to

the edge of her room and looked down. Her
bedroom was flying! Far below Elinor could see
a vast grey desert, pitted with craters. Then
down and down her bedroom went until –
bump! – it landed, sending up a cloud of dust.

Elinor stood at the edge of her bedroom,
coughing and waiting for the dust to settle. Then
she heard a sound. It sounded like long, slow
footsteps.

'Hello?' said Elinor, peering into the dust.
'Who's there?'

Out of the dust cloud came a man. He wore a
silver suit with silver boots and a helmet with a
window in the front. With each step, he rose
slowly into the air, then landed gently, like a
deep-sea diver walking on the bottom of the sea.
He came right up to the edge of Elinor's room
then clumped in across the threshold and took
his helmet off. 'Whew!' His face was flushed and

45

his hair was pressed damply to his head. 'I'm Niall,' he said, and he took off one of his gloves and shook Elinor by the hand. 'Boy, am I glad to see you.'

'I'm Elinor,' said Elinor. 'Would you like a drink of water?'

'No, thanks,' said Niall. 'I've got some juice here.' He sat down in Elinor's wicker chair, took out a small foil packet which he pierced with a straw, and sucked until it rattled. Then he looked around.

'Neat little ship you've got here. Air's pretty fresh, too.'

'Thanks,' said Elinor.

Niall got up and went round her room picking things up and putting them down again. He twirled Elinor's globe, tickled his cheek with a seagull's feather, and pressed Elinor's largest seashell to his ear. Then he turned to Elinor and said, 'So – do you think you can fix it?'

'Fix what?' said Elinor.

'My rocket.'

'Your rocket?'

'Yes! That's why you're here, isn't it?'

Elinor stared at Niall's boots and helmet and his silver suit. He couldn't be… Could he?

Elinor went to her window and opened the curtains – and gasped. For there, thinly wreathed in cloud and turning slowly in space like a blue-green Christmas bauble, was planet Earth.

Her bedroom was on the moon!

'Is something wrong?' said Niall.

'No!' said Elinor. 'It's just … I've never been this far from home before.'

'Me neither,' said Niall. He joined her at the window and they were silent for a moment. Then Elinor said, 'The sea is so blue, isn't it?'

'Yes,' said Niall. 'And the grass is so much *greener* there.'

'I expect it's all the rain,' said Elinor.

'Ah, yes! The rain. Marvellous, isn't it? The way it keeps on coming. Watering the plants and rinsing the pavements and filling up the bird baths and dripping on … on…' Suddenly Niall let out a sob. Elinor handed him a tissue. 'I'm sorry,' he said. 'It's just that – it's only when you're far away you see how beautiful it is.'

'Yes,' said Elinor. She was thinking about the sun shining sideways through the clouds over

Aberdovey estuary, and about the scent of wet
bracken blowing down from the hills – and then
she needed a tissue as well.

'Don't worry,' said Elinor, blowing her nose.
'We'll soon get you home.'

'Know a lot about rockets, do you?'

'A bit,' said Elinor. She went to her bookshelf,

took down a book on rockets and thumbed through the pages. Then she said, 'Have you tested the supersonic nozzle?'

'Fully functional,' said Niall.

'What about the electrostatic ion thrusters?'

'Not responding.'

Elinor nodded. 'Insufficient detonation, I expect. I'd better take a look.'

'You'll need my suit,' said Niall. He took off his silver space suit and his boots and his gloves, and Elinor put everything on. Then she took the alarm clock off her bedside table and slipped it into her pocket.

The moment she left her bedroom she was as light as a birthday balloon. She crossed the ground in huge leaps, sending up a puff of dust with every step.

When she got to the rocket, Elinor opened a panel in the side, took out two small batteries,

and replaced them with the ones from her alarm

clock. Then she bounded slowly back across the

surface of the moon. Niall was standing in his

long johns, waiting.

'That should do it,' said Elinor, clumping in

across the carpet.

'Oh, thank you! Thank you!' cried Niall.

'No problem,' said Elinor. She took off the

space suit and the gloves and boots and Niall put

them on again.

'Goodbye!' he said.

'Goodbye!'

Elinor watched Niall return to his rocket.

After what seemed a very long time, there was a

'whumph!' and the rocket shot straight upwards

like a firework. It curved towards planet Earth

until it was just a small orange speck in the sky –

then disappeared completely.

Elinor was alone. She looked around. Above, behind, below and all around her, empty space went on and on forever. Everyone that Elinor knew, and everyone who had ever been, was up there on that little blue-green marble.

Elinor suddenly longed to get home too. So she stepped off the edge of her bedroom, put her fingers underneath it and lifted. Her whole room was as light as a cardboard box, and floated just above the ground. Then Elinor put her weight against it and pushed. Slowly it began to move. Faster and faster it went until Elinor was running to keep up, and then – *hup!* – she jumped aboard.

Elinor switched on her hairdryer and stood at the edge of her bedroom blasting hot air at the ground. With an explosion of dust her bedroom started rising. Higher and higher it went until the moon was no bigger than a golf ball shining in the darkness below. Then Elinor switched her dryer to HIGH and set her course for planet Earth.

The Flying Bedroom
and the Pirates

On Saturday the weather was wild. Rain ran along the gutters in little rivers. Waves crashed up against the sea wall, soaking people walking their dogs along the promenade.

'What a day!' said Elinor's mother.

'I wouldn't like to be at sea in *this*,' said Elinor's father.

It was still raining when Elinor went to bed. For a long time she lay awake, listening to the rain patter on the windows and the wind trying to get in under the eaves. But eventually, she fell asleep. And while Elinor slept, her bedroom flew.

Up and down and round and round went Elinor's bedroom. The curtains cracked and snapped like washing on the line. Elinor's books all slid to one end of the shelf and several crayons rolled off the edge of her bedroom and were lost forever. Then down, down, down went Elinor's room until – *bump!* – it landed, throwing Elinor out of bed.

Elinor picked herself up. It was still dark, and the rain was blowing crosswise overhead. Elinor switched on her bedside light, put on her dressing gown and rabbit slippers, and went to the edge of her room. In the moonlight she could see waves crashing on the shore and rushing up the sand. Her bedroom was on Aberdovey beach!

But what was this? A rowing boat was coming through the breakers, with two men pulling at the oars. When they reached the shore the men jumped out and dragged their rowboat up onto the sand. Then they lifted out a wooden chest and carried it up the beach towards Elinor's bedroom. One of the men had a wooden leg. The other had an eye patch and a huge black beard.

'Pirates!' whispered Elinor.

The pirates came straight into Elinor's bedroom and dumped the chest on the carpet. Then they slapped each other on the back, linked arms and did a little jig.

'Let's take a look at the loot!' said the pirate with the wooden leg.

'Aye-aye!' said the pirate with the eye patch.

So the pirate with the wooden leg brought across the lamp from Elinor's bedside table, and held it above the trunk. The pirate with the eye patch took a gold key from his pocket. But just as he was just about to put it in the lock the pirate with the wooden leg said, 'Not so fast!' and jerked his thumb at Elinor. 'What about her?'

The pirates looked at Elinor.

'She's only small,' said the pirate with the wooden leg. 'And there's only one of her. We could always…' He drew a finger across his throat.

'So we could,' said the pirate with the eye patch.

'Or,' said the pirate with the wooden leg, 'we could make her promise not to tell.'

'We could indeed.'

So the pirate with the wooden leg turned to Elinor and said, 'Do you promise not to tell anyone?'

'Tell anyone what?' said Elinor.

'About the loot!'

'What loot?' said Elinor. '*I* haven't seen any loot.'

The pirates looked at one another. 'She's right,'
said the pirate with the eye patch. 'She hasn't
seen it yet, has she?'

'No,' said the pirate with the wooden leg. 'She
hasn't. And if she knows what's good for her, she
never will.'

So the pirate with the eye patch went up close
to Elinor. His one eye glittered. 'Two little words,'
he said. '*DON'T LOOK!*'

'I'm not looking,' said Elinor.

'You want to, though, don't you?'

'No.'

'What – not even a tiny bit?'

'Nope,' said Elinor, and she turned away to
rearrange the books upon her shelf.

The pirates looked at one another in surprise.

'Fine,' said the pirate with the wooden leg. 'Don't look, then.'

'Don't worry. I won't!'

'Good!'

The pirate with the patch put the gold key in the lock and waggled it.

Nothing happened.

'Let me have a go,' said the pirate with the wooden leg.

But he couldn't do it either. Eventually they turned to Elinor. 'Excuse me,' they said. 'Would you mind…?'

So Elinor took the key and twisted it the other way. At once the lid flew back revealing golden coins – hundreds of them.

'We're rich! Rich!' cried the pirates. They linked arms and did a little jig. Then the pirate with the wooden leg took out one gold coin and turned it this way and that under the lamp.

Outside the wind roared and rattled at the
windows as though it was trying to get in.

'I bet you'd love to get your hands on these,
wouldn't you?' said the pirate to Elinor.

'Not really,' said Elinor.

'What – not even one?'

'No.'

'Don't be like that,' said the pirate with the eye
patch. 'Have this one. Go on.'

'No thanks. I'm not—'

'TAKE IT!' roared the pirate.

'All right! All right!' said Elinor. 'Keep your hair on.' She took the coin and dropped it into the pocket of her dressing gown.

'Now, then,' said the pirate with the wooden leg. 'We'll share the rest of it between us. Half for me and half for you.'

'Or,' said the pirate with the eye patch. 'Half for me and half for you.'

'Exactly.'

The pirates rolled up their sleeves and plunged their arms into the chest – but their heads met in the middle with a hollow 'clack' and they both sat down abruptly.

Elinor laughed.

The pirates roared and struggled to their feet again. The pirate with the eye patch slapped the other pirate's face. The pirate with the wooden leg yanked on the other pirate's beard.

'Cut it out!' said Elinor.

The pirate with the wooden leg kicked the pirate with the eye patch. The pirate with the eye patch grabbed the other pirate's wooden leg and made him hop in circles.

'Stop it!' said Elinor.

The pirates blundered round Elinor's bedroom, crashing into the furniture and knocking things off the shelves. And all the while the storm raged on outside.

'You're going to break something!' yelled Elinor.

The pirates ignored her. The pirate with the wooden leg snatched the other pirate's eye patch and let go suddenly. The pirate with the eye patch thumped the other pirate with his plastic sword. Outside the wind howled.

'Right,' said Elinor. 'That's it!'

While the pirates carried on fighting, Elinor slammed the lid of the treasure chest, took hold of one of the handles and heaved it out onto the sand.

The weather was wild! But Elinor dragged the chest right down to the edge of the sea. Then she pushed it into the water.

With the first wave, the chest was afloat. The next wave drew it further out. Elinor watched until the treasure chest was just a small dark square bobbing on the waves. Then she marched back to her bedroom, put her fingers in her mouth and whistled.

The pirates stared at her. Then they stared at the place where their treasure chest had been.

'Where's our loot?' they roared.

Elinor pointed at the sea.

With a cry of dismay the pirates ran down the beach, pushed their boat back into the waves, jumped in and began pulling at the oars.

'Bye!' said Elinor.

Soon the boat was just a small dark shape upon the sea – then it was gone. And the storm had retreated, too. The wind had fallen, the rain had stopped, and the night sky was full of stars. Elinor gave a sigh of relief. 'At last,' she said. 'Peace and quiet.' She took the coin out of her pocket, peeled back the gold foil and popped the chocolate disc into her mouth. Then she took off her dressing gown and rabbit slippers, and climbed back into bed. And eventually, lulled by the rush and sigh of the sea, Elinor slept.

When Elinor woke up, it was morning. The
storm had passed. The sun was shining, the
seagulls were soaring high over Aberdovey,
mewing like cats – and the sea was twinkling
more than diamonds.

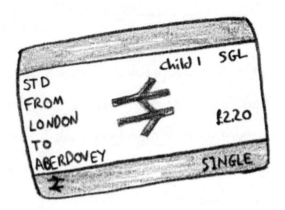

The Flying Bedroom and the Train

Once, Elinor woke up to find her whole room rattling.

She sat up. The tassels on her bedside light were swinging back and forth, and the water in her glass was trembling. And what was that rumbling noise?

Clickety-click-clack went the wheels on the track.

Choo! Choo! went the whistle.

Elinor went to the window and looked out. To her surprise, she saw a rocky coastline rushing past. The clifftops were covered in pink flowers and the sea was crashing on the rocks below.

Elinor put on her dressing gown and rabbit slippers and opened her bedroom door. But instead of the upstairs corridor, Elinor found herself in the corridor of a train. Through the windows on the other side she could see fields of sheep rushing past, and several other carriages curving along the track ahead.

Elinor stepped back into her room and shut the door.

The train was slowing. The brakes squealed and the train came to a stop beside a lonely platform. A woman with a backpack got onto the train, then the door slammed, a whistle blew, and the train pulled off again.

A moment later Elinor's door opened and the woman appeared. 'Hello!' she said. 'Is this a private carriage?'

'No!' said Elinor. 'It's—'

'Oh, good!' The woman took off her backpack and sat down opposite Elinor. 'Hello,' she said. 'I'm Elinor.'

'But that's my name!' said Elinor.

'Call me Ellie, then. Everyone does. Have you come far?'

'I don't know,' said Elinor. 'I just woke up, and here I was.'

Ellie laughed. 'That's the best thing about travelling: waking up somewhere new each day. Isn't it marvellous?'

'But I've got to get back. I've got school in the morning.'

'Don't worry too much about that,' said Ellie. 'You'll reach your destination in the end. We all

do. In the meantime, enjoy the journey.
Sandwich?'

'Thank you,' said Elinor.

Ellie unpacked a cheese and pickle sandwich
and gave half to Elinor, and when Elinor next
looked out of the window she saw that the train

had left the coast behind and was passing
through a dark pine forest.

'Are you going far?' asked Elinor.

'No idea! I just keep going until I feel like
stopping.'

'Really? Where have you been?'

'Where haven't I been?' said Ellie. As they ate
their sandwiches she told Elinor about the time she
had sailed around the Cape, lived in a treehouse in
the Amazon, and built an igloo with the Inuit.

'Don't you get homesick?' asked Elinor.

'Not me!' said Ellie. 'The way I see it, it seems
a shame to stay in one place all your life when
there's a world out there, waiting to be explored.'

'I suppose it does,' said Elinor.

The train was climbing now, and they could
see snow-capped peaks in the distance. It was
getting chilly. Snow was falling on the silent
pines. Elinor put on her winter coat and woolly

hat and scarf. Ellie unpacked a flask of hot chocolate and poured them each a cup.

Presently, the train stopped and three skiers got out of a carriage further down. Then a door banged, the whistle blew, and the train pulled off again.

Elinor sighed. 'I wish I could go travelling too,' she said.

'You will, one day.'

Down the mountainside went the train, faster and faster, and from the window they could see steep ravines with raging rivers crossed by narrow rope bridges. It was getting warmer now, so Elinor took off her coat and hat and scarf and put on her sunglasses. When she sat back down she saw that they were passing through fields of tea bushes, where women were picking leaves and putting them in baskets on their backs.

But soon the train was slowing down and pulling into a busy station. Doors banged, the whistle blew – then in came several women wearing saris. They piled their cases on top of Elinor's wardrobe, and sat in a row on Elinor's bed. Then the whistle blew, and the train pulled off.

The women chattered in a language that Elinor didn't understand, but Ellie passed round a bag of salted peanuts, and the women shared their sticky gulab jamun, and one of the women gave Ellie and Elinor a red dot on their foreheads with her thumb.

But soon the train was slowing and the women in the saris packed up their things, collected their bags, and all got off again.

CLICKETY-CLICK-CLACK went the wheels on the track.

Choo! Choo! went the whistle.

Elinor found a pack of playing cards in her top drawer, and she and Ellie played snap and ate fruitcake. The train passed through shanty towns with houses made of corrugated iron, and then it crossed a bridge over a wide brown river, and they saw water buffalo wading in rice paddies.

The train was stopping again. Four children in school uniform got on the train. They sat in a row on Elinor's bed and got out their recorders, so Elinor got out her recorder too, and they played a tune.

At the next stop the children gathered up their things and left.

CLICKETY-CLICK-CLACK went the wheels on the track.

Choo! Choo! went the whistle.

Every time the train stopped, people got on and people got off. It was hotter now. The train was crossing a wide plain, dotted with acacia trees. They saw a giraffe drinking from a waterhole, and a leopard sleeping in a tree. Then – *whump!* – Elinor's bedroom was plunged into darkness. It rattled and shook and then – *whoosh!* – the train came out of the tunnel again. Now it was passing between tall office blocks, and it was raining.

Ellie began packing up her things. 'I'm getting off here,' she said. 'Enjoy your journey, Elinor.'

'You too,' said Elinor.

They hugged. Then Ellie shouldered her backpack and headed for the door.

'Bye!' said Elinor. She leaned out of the

window and waved at Ellie until she was out of sight. Then she sat back down and opened a book.

Just then, her door opened again and in came a businessman. He put his umbrella in Elinor's wastepaper basket, hung his coat on the back of the door, and sat down opposite. Then he got his newspaper out.

'Hello,' said Elinor.

The man glanced at Elinor over his paper. 'Hello,' he said.

'Are you going far?' asked Elinor.

'Dulwich,' said the man. He noted Elinor's sunglasses, the red dot on her forehead, and her dressing gown. Then he said, 'And you?'

'I don't know,' said Elinor. 'I just keep going until I feel like stopping.'

'Really? Where have you been?'

'Where *haven't* I been?' said Elinor, and she told the man from Dulwich about the snowy mountain tops and the deep ravines and the tea pickers and the leopard in the tree.

The man sighed. 'I wish I could go travelling, too.'

'Why don't you, then?' said Elinor. 'The way I see it, it seems a shame to stay in one place all your life when there's a world out there, waiting to be explored.'

'You know,' said the man, 'you're absolutely right.' He got up and collected his umbrella and his coat.

'Where are you going?' asked Elinor.

'To see the world!' said the man.

Then he was gone.

The train was slowing. Through the window Elinor could see a brick wall sliding past. That was curious, she thought. Then there came an announcement, 'NEXT STOP: EMBANKMENT!' and the train pulled up beside a crowded underground platform. Elinor saw the man from Dulwich get off the train, cross the platform, and leap onto a train going in the opposite direction. A moment later her bedroom door flew open and a crowd of people poured in.

There was a woman with a toddler in a pushchair, a man with a guide dog and a boy wearing headphones. They sat in a line on Elinor's bed, and were joined by a woman reading a book and a girl chewing gum. A very tall man went to the middle of Elinor's bedroom

and held on to the lampshade to steady himself – and several others crowded in around him. Soon there was standing room only. Then the doors closed and the train moved on again.

Every time the train stopped people got on and people got off: PICCADILLY CIRCUS … VICTORIA STATION … EUSTON SQUARE … until eventually, Elinor was alone again. She looked out of the window. Evening had fallen. It had stopped raining and Elinor could see back gardens. The lights were on in kitchen windows. Suddenly Elinor longed to be at home again.

Then the door opened and a conductor appeared. 'Tickets, please!'

'How much to Aberdovey?' asked Elinor.

'Two pounds twenty.'

So Elinor counted out the money in her piggy bank and the conductor printed her a ticket.

'Thank you,' said Elinor.

When he had gone Elinor closed the curtains, hung up her dressing gown, took off her rabbit slippers, and climbed into bed. And soon, lulled by the rocking of the train, Elinor fell asleep.

In the middle of the night, Elinor woke up. Her bedroom had stopped.

She got out of bed and went to the window. The moon was bright. The rooftops of Aberdovey were shining in the moonlight – and faintly, in the distance, Elinor could hear the train: *Clickety-clack-clack. Choo! Choo!* And there it was, pulling out of Aberdovey station.

There was a big world out there, thought Elinor. One day she would get on board that train again.

She watched until it had rounded the
headland and disappeared. Then she yawned,
and got back into bed again.

Also from *Firefly*

Dragon Gold by Shoo Rayner
9781910080047

Steve's Dreams: Steve and the Sabretooth Tiger
by Dan Anthony, illustrated by Huw Aaron
9781910080061

Come to our website for games,
puzzles and competitions.
www.firefly.co.uk

Coming soon:
Pete and the Five-A-Side Vampires by Malachy Doyle,
Dottie Blanket and the Hilltop by Wendy Meddour
and Arthur and Me by Sarah Todd Taylor.